WITHDRAWN

SONG OF SEDNA

SONG OF SEDNA

adapted by Robert D. San Souci

illustrated by Daniel San Souci

A DOUBLEDAY BOOK FOR YOUNG READERS

To our parents

A Doubleday Book for Young Readers
Published by Delacorte Press
Bantam Doubleday Dell Publishing Group, Inc.
1540 Broadway, New York, New York 10036

Doubleday and the portrayal of an anchor with a dolphin
are trademarks of
Bantam Doubleday Dell Publishing Group, Inc.

Library of Congress Cataloging in Publication Data
San Souci, Robert.
Song of Sedna.
SUMMARY: Retells one of many versions of how an
Eskimo maiden became goddess of the sea.
1. Eskimos—Legends.   [1. Eskimos—Legends]
I. San Souci, Daniel.   II. Title.
E99.E7S316   398.2′08997 [E]   80-627
ISBN 0-385-15866-1

Hardcover Reissued June 1994

1   3   5   7   9   10   8   6   4   2

WOR

According to Eskimo myth, Sedna is the goddess of the sea who aids fishermen and hunters.

This book tells one of the many versions of the story of how an Eskimo maiden was transformed into the goddess of the sea.

In the old days, when people were different than they are now, a young Eskimo woman named Sedna lived beside the Arctic Ocean. She was the only daughter of Noato the hunter, whose wife had died when Sedna was born.

Sedna was so beautiful that young men came from near and far to court her. But she was attracted to none of them, and so she refused to marry.

"You must choose a husband soon, my daughter," her father warned, "before word of your fickleness keeps all the young men away."

Sedna answered, "One day the man I have seen in my dreams will come for me. I will not refuse him."

The old man Noato simply shook his head and despaired that his daughter would ever marry. Sedna was strong-willed; more so than her father, whose courage often failed him.

While Sedna waited for the man who was to be her husband, she often wandered with her husky, Setka, who had the blood of the wolf in him. She had raised him from a pup.

Then one day a handsome young hunter arrived from a far-off land. He was dressed in splendid furs and carried a harpoon carved from a single whalebone. The prow of his umiak was unlike those of Sedna's people: It was carved like the head of a serpent.

"My name is Mattak," the stranger said. "Word of your beauty has reached my homeland. Come away with me and be my bride."

Though Sedna recognized him as the man she had dreamed about, she hesitated, for it seemed, as he spoke, that clouds suddenly raced across the sky and a chilling wind arose out of nowhere to whisper a warning in her ear.

Her dog, Setka, broke his tether and ran away.

"What will you offer me to leave my father's igloo behind?" she asked.

He answered, "You shall be mistress of my home on the Island of Birds. There the lamp is always filled with oil, and the pot, with meat."

Sedna was excited by the stranger's promises, but she wished her father was not away hunting so that he could advise her.

"I will give you necklaces of ivory," Mattak continued, "and warm bearskins to rest on. The birds will wake you gently and sing you to sleep."

Feeling as though she moved in a dream, Sedna put aside her doubts and held out her hand to her suitor. With a cry of joy he grasped it and led her toward his umiak, which sat like a giant gull on the shore.

Sedna wished to take her dog with her, but though she called and called, Setka would not return.

She was sad to leave her home behind, but Mattak was anxious to depart. Together they set out across the cloudy and wind-tossed sea.

When Noato returned home, he saw the umiak in the distance. He turned away because the sight grieved him so. He feared that he would never again see his only child.

Sedna and the hunter paddled for five days across a sea grown dark and strange. Sedna often found herself thinking that she had been moving—and continued to move—in a dream. Her companion spoke hardly at all. For much of the time Sedna had only the sound of the wind, the distant cry of birds, and the splash of the waves against the hull to keep her company.

On the sixth day, they entered a harbor guarded by giant polar bears. Sedna was frightened by the beasts, but Mattak told her not to be afraid. His voice calmed her, so that even when one bear reared back and roared, Sedna did not cry out.

They landed in a place where flocks of birds wheeled overhead and thronged the shores and covered the cliff faces in robes of feathered bodies. It seemed to Sedna that the very sun was darkened by the number of birds.

Sedna was amazed to discover that Mattak's home was merely a cave amid the tumbled stones and snow.

Using the snow knife she had brought with her, Sedna showed her husband how to carve out heavy blocks of ice and build a proper igloo. They packed the cracks between the blocks with snow to keep the wind out and bored a hole in the topmost ice block to let warm air escape.

True to his word, Mattak supplied his new wife with more hides and food than she had ever seen before.

She scraped and tanned the skins and gathered soft feathers from the bird cliffs to line the garments she sewed.

Sedna's life was rich and comfortable, but there were times when, alone at her sewing, she became as troubled as the winds and shadows that plagued this otherwise peaceful land.

There came a day when Mattak went on a hunt and forgot his lucky amulet, a bit of ivory carved like a raven's foot.

Sedna followed for a long time in the direction her husband had gone. As she rounded an outcropping of rock and ice, Sedna saw her husband a little way ahead of her. Suddenly she drew back and hid as she saw him change shape. Mattak grew huge wings and soared into the sky. Instantly she knew the truth: She had wed a bird-spirit, an enchanted being who could sometimes take human form.

The young woman fled back to her igloo in fear and confusion. Haunted by the knowledge that she had married a nonhuman, she wept and wondered what to do.

Meanwhile, her father, Noato, who had grown increasingly lonely, had decided to follow his daughter to the Island of Birds. He called his friend the angakok, shaman, who put a blessing on Noato's umiak and told the old man a magic formula to keep his boat safe.

After a long journey, Noato, who had nearly fainted with terror as he passed the huge polar bears, arrived on the island. He found his daughter, filled with grief, pacing the shore. When Sedna told him her husband's secret, Noato insisted that she come away with him.

Sedna agreed this was the best plan, so they put out to sea as quickly as possible, for they were both fearful of the wrath of her demon-husband.

When Mattak returned and discovered that his wife had fled, at first he wept and raged, then he set out in pursuit. His anger and his demon strength enabled him to paddle swiftly through the water.

Soon he came within shouting distance of Noato's boat and cried, "Return Sedna to me!"

Sedna and Noato refused to listen and kept paddling. Then Mattak transformed his own umiak into a huge sea serpent with demon-fire blasting from its jaws.

The angakok's blessing and the magic words Noato had learned kept them always a little ahead of the pursuing monster.

When he saw that he could not overtake them, Mattak gave a tremendous cry of rage. The father and daughter, fearfully looking back, saw a huge bird-shape astride the dragon. Then Mattak's immense wings spread across the sky. Noato and Sedna dared look no longer, but put all their strength into their rowing.

The beating of the giant wings was like thunder. The huge body of the bird blackened the sky like massed storm clouds. There came a shrill cry which grew into the sound of a terrifying storm sweeping across the ocean.

Noato repeated his magic formula, but it was less effective now, because magic loses its power by being used. Seeing this, Noato's courage failed him utterly.

The wind boomed around the tiny boat; waves, rising up, clamored, "Return Sedna to us!"

Convinced that he had offended spirits of sea and storm, Noato hurled his daughter from the boat as a sacrifice to quiet the unearthly voices howling on all sides.

Three times Sedna attempted to climb back into the boat, and each time her fainthearted father pushed her away, crying, "We have offended very great spirits. They call you back, and I must make peace with them."

Exhausted, finally, Sedna gave up the struggle and sank down to the bottom of the sea. A powerful blessing was on her, so she was able to breathe water as if it were air and walk across the floor of the sea as if she were still on dry land.

Two banded seals came and swam above her. In voices as soft as their furred skin, they told her, "Approach that mountain and you will find your destiny."

Sedna guessed that these were really seal-spirits, so she set out toward a mountain of blue ice and ivory in the distance.

On her way she crossed a part of the Kingdom of the Dead. Ghostly shapes on all sides urged her to forsake her journey and rest with them.

"Close your ears," advised the first seal-spirit.

"Your destiny lies ahead of you," the other said.

Sedna drew upon her inner strength and ignored the ghost-voices that called out to her to join them.

Suddenly Sedna encountered a killer whale so ferocious-looking she cried out, "Alas!" and stopped.

But her spirit-guides urged her forward.

The first said, "Have courage."

And the second told her, "Climb upon his back, and he will carry you toward the mountain."

Though she was afraid, she made herself take a step toward the whale. The creature twisted and watched her with eyes as cold as ice chips, but it made no move to attack her.

She put a hand out and discovered that the whale's skin was as ridged as the face of a very old person. Using her hands and feet she climbed onto the back of the beast, which then rose from the sea floor so swiftly that the girl thought she would be swept off as the water rushed past.

The whale carried her most of the way to the mountain, but stopped at the edge of a huge abyss. Across the bottomless canyon arched a bridge as slender as a knife blade.

"This is the last task," said one seal-spirit.

"You must cross the bridge on foot," said the other.

Balancing carefully, Sedna made her way across the delicate bridge, which ended some distance away from the mountain and high above the sea floor.

Urged by the seal-spirits, she swam down and reached the mountain of blue ice and ivory. There she found a throne waiting for her on the highest peak.

All the creatures of the sea gathered around her—walruses, whales, seals, and a multitude of fish—and they proclaimed her goddess of the sea. They promised to obey her every command.

When Sedna was seated upon the throne on the mountain peak, the seal-spirits swam up to her.

The first said to her, "Now anything you wish is in your power."

"But use your power wisely," the second warned, "for a god uses power tempered by wisdom and mercy."

Sedna realized that she was being tested. She sensed that her powers might be taken from her if she misused them. So she followed the best instincts of her heart.

She moved her hands, and power flowed from them. She became, for a moment, one with the waters and caused them to swallow up the igloo where her father lay sleeping near her dog, Setka.

When the old man and dog had been pulled beneath the waves, the seal-spirits brought them before Sedna, who had returned to her throne upon the mountain.

Noato trembled to see the change in his daughter, for her power shone all around her. He was sure she would punish him for having thrown her from the boat so heartlessly.

But Sedna, who felt the force and rightness of her destiny, forgave her father and made a home for him in the land beneath the sea. She made Setka special guardian of her throne.

Her actions pleased Silarssuaq, the great spirit of justice, who is the most powerful being of all.

From the bottom of the Arctic Ocean, Sedna reigns to this day as goddess of the sea. The Eskimos seek her goodwill whenever they need protection on the open sea or help with harvesting the sea's bounty.

They say that sometimes, when the sea wind blows a certain way, you can hear the voice of Sedna singing:

> "My joy
> Rises from the depths of the sea like bubbles
> That burst in the light;
> My song
> Is a promise for the winds to carry
> To everyone who lives by the sea."

Robert and Daniel San Souci together have published many award-winning books, including The Legend of Scarface—a New York Times Best Illustrated Book—The Legend of Sleepy Hollow, The Christmas Ark, and Feathertop.

While continuing to collaborate, the brothers also produce works independently. Robert's Larger Than Life received wide acclaim. School Library Journal said, "Text and illustrations are exuberant. . . . This collection will practically leap from the shelf into many an eager hand." Daniel's North Country Night was selected as a Pick of the Lists by American Bookseller, which named it "one of the outstanding books of the season . . . soft and tender yet compellingly realistic."

Both Robert and Daniel San Souci live in the San Francisco Bay area.